LITTLE RICKY EXPLORES
ITALY

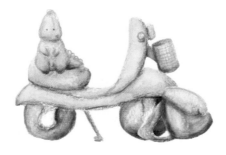

WRITTEN BY ELISA McALPINE   ILLUSTRATED BY MARIA KIRSHINA

PUBLISHED IN 2019 BY ELISA MCALPINE

ILLUSTRATED BY MARIA KIRSHINA

FOR MY SON, IBRAHIM. MAY YOU GROW INTO A KIND AND LOVING MAN WHO SEES THE BEAUTY THIS WORLD HAS TO OFFER.

BENVENUTI!
WELCOME TO ITALY!

LET'S FIRST EXPLORE
THE ISLAND OF SICILY.

It has a volcano
and beaches too.
Let's go for a swim.
The sea is so blue!

OFF TO CATANIA.
A MOST MARVELOUS CITY!
LET'S SEE THE PIAZZA DEL DUOMO
WITH A CATHEDRAL SO PRETTY!

Now onto the boot.
Where the mainland starts.
Let's take the ferry
as we part.

ON OUR WAY TO NAPLES
I HEAR A RUMBLE IN MY TUMMY.

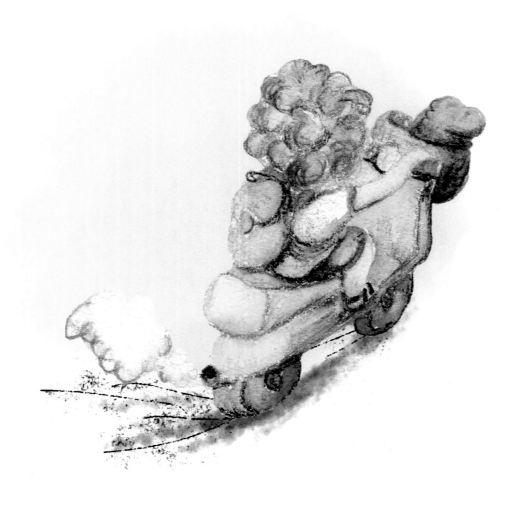

STOPPING FOR SOME PIZZA.
MMMMMM SO YUMMY!

Now it's off to Pompeii!
A city underground.
Let's take a tour to see
all the treasures that were found!

OFF TO ROME!
TO THE COLOSSEUM WE MUST GO.

AND WHEN WE'RE DONE
WE'LL GET SOME GELATO!

THEN OVER TO PISA
TO SEE THE TOWER.
ON OUR WAY
WE SEE MANY FLOWERS.

NEXT IS VENICE.
IT'S A CITY ON WATER.
TAKE A GONDOLA FOR A RIDE,
BUT BE CAREFUL, IT MIGHT TOTTER!

LET'S GO SHOPPING IN MILAN!
THEY'RE KNOWN FOR THEIR FASHION.
SO MUCH TO CHOOSE FROM.
IT'S TRULY THEIR PASSION!

Our time here is done,
to home we must go.
Arrivederci, my sweet Italy.
We'll see you again, pronto!

Made in the USA
Middletown, DE
25 March 2023

27625255R00018